Charlie and his Super Powers

It was a beautiful Autumn day in London and the sky was clear. Charlie was lying on his bed reading a book about his favourite football team. Out of his window he could see the blue sky with just a few puffy clouds that looked like big marshmallows.

"Get dressed Charlie" shouted his mum "and brush your teeth".

"Hurry up, we are going to Whipwhip Zoo"

Charlie jumped out of
bed, ran to the bathroom,
grabbed his toothbrush,
quickly put toothpaste on
his toothbrush and
frantically began brushing
his teeth.

Whilst he was brushing his
teeth, Charlie was trying
to brush his hair with the
other hand. He was so
excited that he was trying
to do both at the same time.
If this was not enough, he
tried to sing along as well:

"Im going to Whipwhip
woohoo Whipwhip woohoo"

On the way to the zoo, Charlie's mum told him they were picking up his two best friends on the way.

Max and Charlie had been friends ever since they were in nursery and both decided they wanted the only cricket bat stored in the toy box at nursery. They fought like crazy that first day over the cricket bat and since then they were the best of friends.

Bernie, was in year two with Charlie and Max and although they had not known Bernie long, Bernie had a way of making the boys laugh hysterically and as a result he had quickly become one of their closest friends.

All three boys were very excited to be on the way to the zoo until Charlie's mum made one last stop to collect Charlie's first cousin, Henry!

Henry was always causing chaos wherever he went. He left a trail of destruction behind him and was always getting into trouble whether he was at school or at home.

Often, Henry would do something very naughty and then tell his parents that he and Charlie had done such a deed. As a result Charlie always tried his best to avoid Henry whenever possible.

As they arrived at Whipwhip zoo, the boys could hardly contain their excitement when they saw a large enclosure with a sign, "Beware, do not exit your vehicles in this enclosure".

What animals could be in that enclosure they thought? Was it lions or tigers or maybe large brown or black bears?

The boys couldn't wait to get inside the zoo to explore the different enclosures and to tackle the jungle gyms.

6

Charlie's mum paid the entrance fee and they drove through the gates of Whipwhip and the first sign on the side of the road said " turn right to Africa Land". Charlie's mum turned right and drove 150 metres down the road and parked the car outside the huge sign that read 'Africa Land'. "Come on boys", she shouted, "bring your hats and make sure you put on some sunscreen on your faces".

Everyone grabbed their hats and put on sunscreen, except Henry who refused. So Bernie decided to tickle him on the grass whilst Max and Charlie smeared sunscreen all over his face.

AFRICA
LAND

The first enclosure was at least the size of ten football pitches, it was huge and somewhere in the open there were eight white rhinoceros calmly grazing the very succulent grass. The rhinoceros were quite far away and the boys were standing on the fence enclosure trying to get a better vantage point.

"Lets jump over the fence and run closer" shouted Henry. "Dont be silly Henry, those rhinoceros will charge at you and crash you!" said Charlie. "Exactly" said Max, who was the cleverest boy that Charlie had ever met. "Thats why they call it a crash of rhinos".

Fun facts about White Rhinos

1. THERE ARE FIVE SPECIES OF RHINO IN THE WORLD

These include two African rhino species – black and white rhinos. The remaining three are Asian rhino species, which include greater one-horned, Sumatran and Javan rhinos.

2. RHINOS CAN WEIGH OVER 3 TONNES

Sumatran rhinos are the smallest of all rhinos, but they can still weigh 600kg (that's almost 95 stone). On the other hand, white rhinos are the largest of the rhino species, weighing up to 3,500 kg.

3.BLACK AND WHITE RHINOS ARE BOTH, IN FACT, GREY

The names of black and white rhinos are misleading – as both are actually grey. The white rhino is said to have gotten its name from the Afrikaans word for wide ('wyd'), referring to it's wide, square lip (in contrast, black rhinos have a pointy upper lip).

4. THEY'RE CALLED BULLS AND COWS

Male rhinos are called 'bulls' and females are called 'cows'. Their young are called 'calves'.

5. WHAT ARE RHINO HORNS MADE OF? THE SAME STUFF AS OUR FINGERNAILS

Rhino horn is made up of keratin - the same protein which forms the basis of our hair and nails.

While the boys were still looking at the rhinos,
Henry headed off on his own to go see the giraffe.
These were not regular giraffe, these were
reticulated giraffe from East Africa.

Charlie's mum had noticed that Henry had wandered
off unattended and she told the boys to follow her
to the giraffe enclosure so that they did not lose
Henry. As they were arriving, Charlie spotted
Henry taking some large carrots out of the
handlers basket. Charlie ran up to stop Henry
feeding the giraffe without permission. As soon as
Charlie went to grab the carrots, one of the
giraffes bit the carrot and chomped into
Charlie's finger at the same time.

Charlie let out an almighty scream when he got bitten, which gave the giraffe such a fright that it ran away.

The zoo staff came running to see how Charlie was, he had a bite right on the tip of his finger.

Luckily the bite was not too bad and all it required was some disinfectant and a band aid.
Once again, Charlie had landed himself in trouble thanks to his cousin Henry!

Fun facts about Reticulated Giraffes

1. WHAT TYPE OF ANIMAL IS A RETICULATED GIRAFFE?

Reticulated giraffes are the most well-known among the nine giraffe subspecies. Reticulated giraffes are tall and have stunning white lines making large polygonal shapes.

2. HOW MANY RETICULATED GIRAFFES ARE THERE IN THE WORLD?

There are only 8,700 reticulated giraffes living in the wild.

3. WHAT IS A RETICULATED GIRAFFE'S HABITAT?

Reticulated giraffe habitats are in Northern Kenya, Somalia, and Southern Ethiopia. They live in forests, rainforests, woodlands, savannas, and seasonal floodplains.

4. WHO DO RETICULATED GIRAFFES LIVE WITH?

Reticulated giraffes live together in herds with between ten and 15 individuals. This helps them to survive against predators. They take turns feeding while others look out for danger.

5. HOW LONG DOES A RETICULATED GIRAFFE LIVE?

Reticulated giraffes have an average life span of 25 years when in their natural habitat and about 27 years in captivity.

6. HOW BIG IS A RETICULATED GIRAFFE?

Male reticulated giraffes reach a height of 216 inches (18 ft) and weigh between 2,400-4,250 lb (1,088-1,927 kg). The height of the female can reach up to 204 inches (17 ft) and weigh between 1,540-2,600 lb (689-1,179 kg).

7. HOW FAST CAN A RETICULATED GIRAFFE RUN?

Reticulated giraffes are fast, and they can gallop up to 35 mph (56 kmph).

16

After a fun day, which involved ice cream, hamburgers, hotdogs, cotton candy and loads of climbing and running around the boys were on their way home and exhausted.

When Charlie got home, he headed to his room to clean up before he went to bed. Whilst Charlie was brushing his teeth he started to feel very strange, he was sweating and he didn't feel quite right.

That night, Charlie had very strange dreams. He dreamt he could fly like a bird, he could roar like a lion and he was as strong as an elephant.

When Charlie woke up the next morning, he went downstairs because he was so hungry. Charlie saw his dad reading the newspaper and the headline on page two read:

'Giraffe's food at Whipwhip zoo found to contain radioactive material'.

Charlie didn't think anything of the headline. After breakfast, Charlie and his parents went for a walk on the heath.

Charlie felt strange, like he could hear and smell things that he normally could not. All of a sudden out of nowhere, there were two dogs that jumped out and looked terrifying. They were foaming at the mouth and barking at Charlie and his family and approaching them menacingly.

In a flash, Charlie felt strange and noticed he was changing into an animal, not just any animal but a fully grown brown bear. Charlie stood 3-feet taller than his father and mother, who could not believe what was happening. He let out an almighty growl, which sent the two dogs running with their tails between their legs.

Almost as soon as they had disappeared, Charlie turned back from a bear into a normal boy again. What had just happened?

Fun facts about Brown Bears

1. BROWN BEARS AREN'T JUST BROWN

Some are in fact cream or black.

2. BROWN BEARS ARE OMNIVORES

Which means they eat just about anything. They'll eat deer, fish, small mammals, berries, honey, nuts and plants. They'll eat your rubbish if you let them, but you should never feed a bear.

3. BROWN BEARS DIG COZY CAVES WITH THEIR LONG CLAWS

They sleep in the caves for most of the winter. Their heartbeats slow down to 10 beats per minute.

4. BROWN BEAR MAMMAS HAVE BABIES DURING THE WINTER WHILE THEY ARE ASLEEP!

The babies drink mamma's milk and stay warm in their mamma's fur. In the spring, mamma wakes up to meet her new cubs.

Charlie soon realised that the bite from the giraffe had given him some kind of super power. He was not aware yet what exactly his powers were, but he was soon going to find out.

Charlie had acquired the power to change into any animal or bird he thought of whenever he liked. Charlie could be a lion, an elephant or an eagle. He would soon learn that he could even change himself into a prehistoric animal such as a Tyrannosaurus Rex.

Whilst Charlie was excited about his super powers, his parents were worried that there was something very wrong with him, so they took him straight to the doctor.

The doctor inspected Charlie and could not believe what he was seeing. Charlie's eyesight was as sharp as an eagle, he could read the smallest line on the eye chart from across the room.

He was so strong that when the doctor dropped his stethoscope under the table, Charlie was able to lift the doctor's table with just one finger. When the doctor asked him to take a deep breath so he could listen to his chest, Charlie could hold his breath for ten whole minutes. The doctor could find nothing wrong with Charlie and he was sent home with a clean bill of health.

SCHOOL BUS
27

That next day, Charlie was eating a sandwich and waiting for the school bus to arrive. Charlie jumped on the bus and went to sit with Max and Bernie. On the way to school, the bus driver told all the boys and girls to be seated immediately as the brakes of the bus had failed and he couldn't slow the bus down. Charlie was sitting down, when all of a sudden he started to feel he was changing, he was changing into the biggest python that you have ever seen. Charlie hooked his tail around one of the seats while slithering out of a window and wrapping his head around a large red postbox. Charlie managed to slow the bus down.

Charlie had saved the day and managed to bring the out-of-control bus to a halt. All the kids and the bus driver cheered when they saw what Charlie had done as he had saved them all from a certain accident. Charlie was a real hero.

Fun facts about Pythons

1. PYTHONS ARE NON VENOMOUS SNAKES

They do not use venom to catch their prey. Instead, they belong to the group of snakes called constrictors.

2. WHERE DO YOU FIND PYTHONS?

They are only found in Africa, Asia, and Australia. They inhabit a wide range of habitats. They can live in rainforest, grasslands, woodlands, swamps, mountains, and deserts.

Even in the wild, pythons are one of the longest living species of snakes. They have been found in the wild to have lived up to and over 30 years.

3. **THE LARGEST SPECIES OF PYTHON IS THE RETICULATED PYTHON**

These gigantic snakes have been found in the wild measuring over 30 feet in length and weighing 250 lbs.

4 THE PATTERNS ON EACH OF THE DIFFERENT SPECIES OF PYTHONS VARY DEPENDING UPON THEIR ENVIRONMENT

Most pythons prefer to live in trees, but some will live in abandoned burrows. If a python lives in a tree, it is referred to as arboreal. If they prefer to live on the ground, they are referred to as terrestrial.

5. **HOW DO PYTHONS USE THEIR SENSES?**

Like most snakes, pythons do not have ears. They instead rely on the vibrations they feel on the ground to tell when prey or danger is near.

Pythons also don't smell with their noses like we do. Instead, they use their forked tongues to taste the air.

Later that week at school, Charlie and his schoolmates were so excited as they were going on a school excursion to Buckingham Palace.

On the way from the train station to Buckingham Palace, Henry had distracted some of the teachers and one of the kids, Tom Jeeves, was lost and the teachers were panicking because they couldn't find Tom.

Charlie quickly turned into an eagle and soared into the sky. Not only did he get an amazing view of Buckingham Palace from the sky but he was also able to spot Tom with his excellent vision. Once again Charlie had saved the day and Tom was so glad he had been found that he shared his biscuits that his mother had packed for him with Charlie. Charlie was a real hero.

Fun facts about Fish Eagles

1. THERE ARE SEVEN SPECIES OF FISH EAGLE

2. THERE ARE AROUND 300,000 FISH EAGLES IN AFRICA

3. FISH EAGLES ARE ONE OF THE OLDEST OF ALL LIVING BIRDS

4. THEY ARE KLEPTOPARASITES:

This means they actively steal food from other birds.

5. AFRICAN FISH EAGLES AREN'T JUST SCAVENGERS, NOR DO THEY FEED PURELY ON FISH

Fish is supplemented by other birds and mammals.

6. AFRICAN FISH EAGLES SOMETIMES EAT MONKEYS AND BABY CROCODILES!

7. THEY MATE FOR LIFE

8. THEY GRAB PREY WITH THEIR REMARKABLE FEET AND TALONS

Charlie went to bed that night and slept really well as he was exhausted from all his heroics.

35

36

Charlie Saves Red Rovers

The Adventures of Charlie Winkle

Tony Herbert & Ricky Herbert

Book 2

Join Charlie to see what other incredible adventures he has in store for **you**.